CW00839324

Chickens on a Mission:

A Farmyard Tale

Copyright © 2023 Emma afia. All rights reserved. No part of this publication may be reproduced, stored in a retrieval system, or transmitted in any form or by any means, electronic, mechanical, photocopying, recording, or otherwise, without the prior written permission of the copyright owner. This book is sold subject to the condition that it shall not be resold, lent, hired out or otherwise circulated without the publisher's prior consent in any form of binding or cover other than that in which it is published and without a similar condition including this condition being imposed on the subsequent purchaser.

This is a work of fiction. Names, characters, businesses, organizations, places, events, and incidents either are the product of the author's imagination or are used fictitiously. Any resemblance to actual persons, living or dead, events, or locales is entirely coincidental.

The following trademarked terms are mentioned in this book: Mohamed El Afia. The use of these trademarks does not indicate an endorsement of this work by the trademark owners. The trademarks are used in a purely descriptive sense and all trademark rights remain with the trademark owner.

Cover design by el Emma afia.

This book was typeset in Emma afia.

First edition, 2023.

Published by Emma Afia.

Chapter 1: Boredom on the Farm

- Introduce the main characters: a group of chickens who live on a farm.
- Establish their daily routine of laying eggs and pecking for food.
- Show how they're all feeling bored and unfulfilled with their lives on the farm.

Chapter 2: The Plan

- One of the chickens comes up with a plan to leave the farm and see the world.
- The other chickens are hesitant at first, but eventually agree to join in.
- They work together to come up with a plan and gather supplies for their journey.

Chapter 3: The Great Escape

- The chickens put their plan into action and escape from the farm.
- They face various obstacles and challenges, including crossing a busy road and avoiding predators.
- They finally make it to a nearby town and are amazed by all the sights and sounds.

Chapter 4: Learning and Growing

- The chickens explore the town and have various adventures along the way.
- They learn important lessons about teamwork, perseverance, and friendship.
- They also discover their unique abilities and how they can use them to make a difference in the world.

Chapter 5: Finding their Way Home

- The chickens realize they miss their home on the farm and start to feel homesick.
- They work together to find their way back home, facing new challenges and obstacles along the way.
- They finally make it back to the farm and are welcomed back by their friends and family with open wings. They feel fulfilled and grateful to be back home, but also enriched by their adventure and the lessons they've learned.

Chapter 1: Boredom on the Farm

The sun was rising over the farm, and the rooster let out his familiar crow. The chickens, who were all still nestled in their cozy coop, began to stir. But as they stretched their wings and hopped down to the ground, they couldn't shake the feeling of boredom and unfulfillment.

Henrietta, the leader of the flock, clucked to her friends, "I'm tired of this same old routine every day. Laying eggs, pecking for food, and roosting at night. There must be more to life than this!"

The other chickens murmured their agreement. Hattie complained, "I'm so bored, I could lay an egg!" while Peaches squawked, "I want to do something exciting, like fly to the moon!" Despite their grumbling, the chickens carried on with their daily chores. But the seed of discontent had been planted in their minds, and they couldn't stop thinking about all the adventures and possibilities that lay beyond the farmyard fence.

As the day wore on, the chickens grew increasingly restless and bored. They wandered around the yard, pecking at the ground, but their hearts just weren't in it. Finally, as the sun began to set, Henrietta made a bold declaration. "Enough is enough! We can't go on like this. We need to do something different, something exciting. Who's with me?"

The other chickens hesitated for a moment, unsure of what she was suggesting. But then they looked at each other, and a spark of adventure ignited in their eyes.

"I'm in!" said Hattie.

"Me too!" chimed in Peaches.

And with that, the chickens began to hatch a plan. They were going to leave the farm and see the world beyond.

Chapter 2: The Plan

Excitement buzzed through the group of chickens as they huddled together to plan their escape. Henrietta took charge, as usual, and began laying out their options. "We can't just fly over the fence. We need to find a way to get past the farmer and his watchful eye," she said. Hattie suggested, "What if we dig a tunnel? Like in the movies!"

But Peaches shook her head, "That's a lot of work, and what if we get stuck? I say we go for the direct approach. We just run for it!"

Henrietta considered this for a moment, then nodded. "I think Peaches is right. We'll have to be fast, though. And quiet. The farmer can't see or hear us."

They made a list of things they'd need for the journey: food, water, maps, and a compass. Henrietta assigned each chicken a task, and they got to work gathering supplies.

As night fell and the farm went quiet, the chickens crept out of the coop and made their way to the edge of the yard. They could see the lights of the farmhouse in the distance, and the shadowy form of the farmer patrolling the fields.

"Okay, everyone. This is it," said Henrietta, her voice low. "We need to move fast, and stay together. Ready?"

The chickens took a deep breath and then, as one, they ran towards the fence. They felt their hearts pounding in their chests as they approached the wire mesh. With a mighty leap, they all soared over the top and landed in a heap on the other side.

"Whew, that was close!" said Hattie, as they brushed themselves off.
"Okay, let's go!" said Henrietta, and they set off on their adventure, eager to explore the world beyond the farmyard.

Chapter 3: The Great Escape

The chickens had done it! They had escaped the confines of the farmyard and were now free to explore the world beyond. They ran through the fields, flapping their wings in excitement. "This is amazing!" exclaimed Peaches. "I never knew there was so much open space!"

As they journeyed further, they encountered all sorts of new and exciting things: towering trees, babbling brooks, and even a sparkling pond filled with fish.

But they soon realized that the world beyond the farm was also filled with danger. They encountered a sly fox who tried to catch them for dinner, and narrowly escaped the talons of a hungry hawk.

"We need to be careful," warned Henrietta. "There are predators out here who would love to make a meal of us."

Despite the danger, the chickens persevered. They continued on their journey, crossing fields and forests, scaling hills and mountains.

Finally, after many days of travel, they reached a bustling city. The sights and sounds were overwhelming: honking cars, towering skyscrapers, and people rushing around everywhere.

"Wow, this is so different from the farm!" said Hattie, as they looked around in wonder.

"But how will we find our way around?" asked Peaches, looking worried.

Henrietta stepped forward. "We'll use the maps and compass we brought with us. And we'll work together. We're chickens on a mission, remember?"

And with that, the chickens set off into the city, ready for their next adventure.

Chapter 4: Learning and Growing

As the chickens explored the city, they encountered all sorts of new experiences. They saw towering buildings and busy streets, and heard the sound of cars and buses rushing by. At first, they felt overwhelmed and scared. But Henrietta reminded them that they were chickens on a mission, and that they needed to be brave and keep going.

As they explored, they learned about the different neighborhoods and landmarks of the city. They met friendly people who gave them directions and even offered them food.

The chickens also encountered new types of food, like pizza and hot dogs. They discovered that there was more to life than just corn and grains. They also learned about the importance of staying healthy, as they encountered other animals who were not as lucky.

"I can't believe how much we've learned," said Peaches, as they settled down for the night in a park. "I feel like a whole new chicken!"

"Me too," agreed Hattie. "I never knew there was so much to see and do in the world."

But Henrietta cautioned them not to forget their mission. "We're not just here to explore. We're also here to learn and grow, so that we can bring new ideas back to the farm."

The chickens nodded, understanding the importance of their journey. They went to sleep that night, excited for the adventures that awaited them in the days to come.

Chapter 5: Finding their Way Home

As much as the chickens enjoyed their new experiences in the city, they knew they couldn't stay forever. They missed the familiar sights and smells of the farm, and longed to be back home.

But finding their way back would be no easy task. They had traveled so far, and had no idea how to retrace their steps.

"We need to find a way to get back to the farm," said Henrietta. "But we can't do it alone. We need to ask for help." The chickens spent the next few days talking to people in the city, asking if anyone knew the way back to their farm. Some people laughed at them, thinking they were just silly chickens. But others were kind and helpful, and pointed them in the right direction.

Finally, after many long days of travel, they saw the familiar silhouette of the farm in the distance.

"We made it!" exclaimed Peaches, flapping her wings in excitement.

But as they got closer, they realized something was wrong. The farmer was standing in the yard, looking angry.

"What are you chickens doing here?" he yelled. "You belong in the coop!"

The chickens looked at each other, unsure of what to do. They had come so far, only to be sent back to their boring old lives in the coop. But Henrietta refused to give up. "We're not just chickens," she said, looking the farmer straight in the eye. "We're chickens on a mission. And we've learned so much on our journey. We can make the farm a better place, if you'll let us."

The farmer looked at them for a moment, then nodded. "Alright, you can stay out of the coop. But you'll have to earn your keep. You can start by helping me with the chores."

The chickens smiled, grateful for the opportunity to make a difference. As they settled back into farm life, they knew they would never forget their adventures in the city, and the lessons they had learned along the way.

The End

Copyright © 2023 Emma afia. All rights reserved. No part of this publication may be reproduced, stored in a retrieval system, or transmitted in any form or by any means, electronic, mechanical, photocopying, recording, or otherwise, without the prior written permission of the copyright owner. This book is sold subject to the condition that it shall not be resold, lent, hired out or otherwise circulated without the publisher's prior consent in any form of binding or cover other than that in which it is published and without a similar condition including this condition being imposed on the subsequent purchaser.

This is a work of fiction. Names, characters, businesses, organizations, places, events, and incidents either are the product of the author's imagination or are used fictitiously. Any resemblance to actual persons, living or dead, events, or locales is entirely coincidental.

The following trademarked terms are mentioned in this book: Mohamed El Afia. The use of these trademarks does not indicate an endorsement of this work by the trademark owners. The trademarks are used in a purely descriptive sense and all trademark rights remain with the trademark owner.

Cover design by el Emma afia.

This book was typeset in Emma afia.

First edition, 2023.

Published by Emma Afia.

Printed in Great Britain
by Amazon

38997219R00020